Bats at the Beach

WRITTEN AND ILLUSTRATED BY BRIAN LIES

HOUGHTON MIFFLIN HARCOURT BOSTON NEW YORK

Maddy, this one is all yours.

All rights reserved. Originally published in hardcover in the United States by Houghton Mifflin
Books for Children, an imprint of Houghton Mifflin Harcourt Publishing Company, 2006.

For information about permission to reproduce selections from this book, write to
trade.permissions@hmhco.com or to Permissions, Houghton Mifflin Harcourt Publishing Company, 3 Park Avenue, 19th Floor, New York, New York 10016.

www.hmhco.com

The text of this book is set in 18-point Legacy.
The illustrations are acrylic paint on Strathmore paper.

The Library of Congress has cataloged the hardcover edition as follows:
Lies, Brian.
Bats at the beach/written and illustrated by Brian Lies.
p. cm.
Summary: On a night when the moon can grow no fatter, bats pack their moon-tan lotion and baskets of treats and fly off for some fun on the beach.
[1. Beaches—Fiction. 2. Bats—Fiction. 3. Picnicking—Fiction. 4. Stories in rhyme.] I. Title.
PZ8.3.L5963Bat 2006
[E]—dc22
2005010757

ISBN: 978-0-618-55744-8 hardcover
ISBN: 978-0-544-66840-9 paperback

Manufactured in China
SCP 10 9 8 7 6 5
4500682025

Sun slips down and all is still,
and soon we can't tell sky from hill.
Now from barn and cave and rafter,
bats pour out with shrieks of laughter.

The rising moon can grow no fatter
as sky lights up with gleeful chatter:
Quick, call out! Tell all you can reach—
the moon is just perfect for bats at the beach!

Soon we've got our buckets, trowels,
banjoes, blankets, books, and towels,
strapped on backs and under wings.
—Have we forgotten anything?

Launching out into the breeze,
we sail above the darkened trees,
flying fast, to wet our feet
where land and foamy ocean meet.

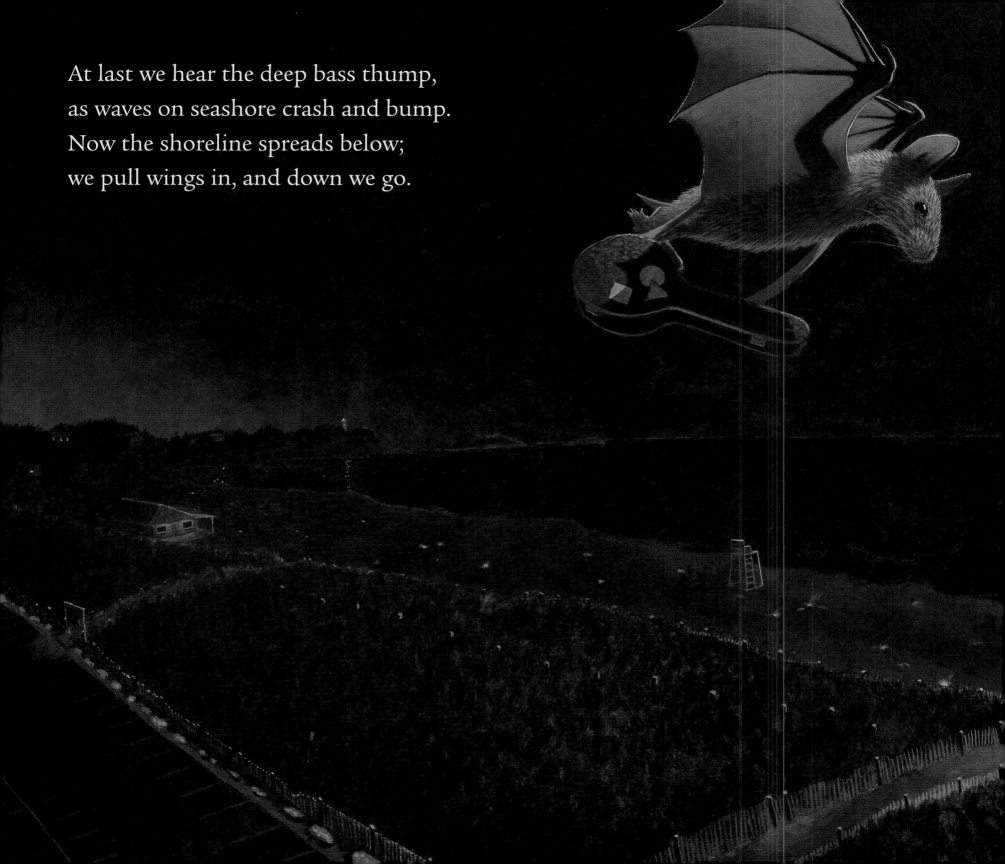

At last we hear the deep bass thump,
as waves on seashore crash and bump.
Now the shoreline spreads below;
we pull wings in, and down we go.

How delicious—oh, how sweet,
To feel warm sand beneath our feet.
Quick, set up—spread blankets on sand!
We want to get going when fun is at hand.

We hurry down to test the ocean.
Don't forget the moon-tan lotion!
What's the first thing we should do?
So many games before night's through.

Like playing with the stuff we find,
which others must have left behind.

Burying friends from chin to knee,
we're scratchy where no sand should be.

Making friends from other places
with different foods and different faces.

Or sailing to terrific heights,
taking turns at being kites.
Little bats dig their sand caves deep,
as old bats lie in the moon, asleep.

There's really no more thrilling ride
than surfing on a summer tide.
Or sailing in the wing-boat races,
with salty sea spray in our faces.

Now it's munchtime; what's to eat?
Baskets groan with yummy treats.
Beetles, ants, and milkweed bugs,
crickets, moths, and pickled slugs.
Damselflies, or salted 'skeeters—
no room *here* for picky eaters!

Bug-mallows toast on slender sticks
while cousins do their ocean tricks.

And later on, though stomachs hurt,
we'll try the snack bar for dessert.

Quick, don't miss it—the old bats are singing
the bat songs that *they* learned
when *they* were first winging!

Music rolls on, but no more games.
As embers pop within the flames,
little ones climb onto leathery lap,
determined to rest but not to nap.

Then east sky purples—sun is coming!
A last few notes of banjo-strumming
bring our beach night to an end,
so say farewell to newfound friends.
Pack our things up, shake the sand out,
give the noisy gulls a handout.

Quick, let's go, let's fly away—
we've got to be home before it's day!

Flutter homeward, drained and weary.
Small bats doze off, tired and teary.

Day birds start to chirp and peep;
now back to crack and crevice creep.
We sigh and snuggle close together
to dream about the moony weather.

Shh—now sleep. The moon's out of reach.
The night was just perfect for bats at the beach.